FRiGHTViLLE

CURSE OF THE WISH EATER

FRIGHTVILLE

CURSE OF THE WISH EATER

BY MIKE FORD

Scholastic Inc.

All rights reserved. Published by Scholastic Inc., *Publishers since 1920*. SCHOLASTIC and associated logos are trademarks and/or registered trademarks of Scholastic Inc.

The publisher does not have any control over and does not assume any responsibility for author or third-party websites or their content.

ISBN 978-1-338-36011-0

10 9 8 7 6 5 4 3 2   20 21 22 23

Printed in the U.S.A.   40
First printing 2019

Book design by Stephanie Yang

FOR JEANNIE

"Did you find something?" Max asked his mother for the fifth time in as many minutes.

For the fifth time she answered, "Not yet, sweetie."

They had been inside the Gingerbread House for what felt like hours. Max's mother was looking for a gift for his aunt Maxine's birthday. They were having a party for her at their house that night, and they'd already been to the grocery store for food, the florist for flowers, the party store for balloons, and the bakery for a cake. The present was the last thing on the list.

"How about this?" Max asked, picking something at random from a shelf and holding it up.

His mother looked at it. "I don't think Aunt Maxine would like a ceramic clown."

Max groaned and put the clown back.

"Why don't you go look around?" his mother suggested. "I won't be much longer."

"There's nothing interesting to look at," Max complained, indicating the shelves filled with candles, teacups, and bubble bath. Nothing a ten-year-old boy would want.

"Why don't you go to that new store that opened next door, then?" his mother said.

"There might be something fun there. I'll be done here in a few minutes and will come meet you, okay?"

"Okay," Max said unenthusiastically. *It will probably be more boring old-lady stuff,* he thought as he walked out of the Gingerbread House.

He peered into the window of the shop next door. The name was painted in red-and-black letters across the glass: FRIGHTVILLE. *Looks like a lot of old junk,* Max thought as he pushed the door open and went inside.

He was wrong. Frightville wasn't filled with junk. Max stood just inside the doorway, marveling at a room overflowing with stuff that most definitely wasn't for old ladies. At least not old ladies like his aunt Maxine.

"You look like a young man who enjoys interesting things," said a voice.

Behind the counter of the shop, a man was standing and regarding Max with an appraising air. Tall and thin, he was wearing a black suit that looked like it was probably a hundred years old. The man himself also looked like he might be a hundred years old, with pale skin and silver hair.

"This is a lot better than teacups," Max remarked.

"Oh, I have some extremely fascinating teacups," the man said, coming out from behind the counter. "They tell your fortune. But I have a feeling you're looking for something *really* special."

Max grinned. "What have you got?" he asked.

The man waved his hands around. "See for yourself," he said. "Adventure waits around every corner." He paused, raising one eyebrow. "For those who aren't afraid to look for it," he concluded.

Max wandered around the store—checking out everything. The man was right—there *were* teacups. But there were so many other things. There was a doll that was sewn out of scraps of different-patterned fabrics, a jar filled with antique keys that looked like they might unlock treasure chests, and lots of boxes with peculiar symbols on their sides that made Max wonder what might be inside them. But then he saw something *really* weird. Tucked into the dusty corner of a cupboard was a set of teeth. Max tapped his fingernail against them. He'd thought they might be wood or plastic, but they actually felt like real teeth. Or maybe they were ivory or bone. Whatever they were made of, they were old and stained, and there was a small metal key sticking out of one side. Max picked the teeth up and discovered that there was a paper tag tied to the key. Written on the tag was a short poem:

The Wish Eater

Make a wish and write it down

Place it in the Eater's mouth

Go away, come back and check

If it's gone, the answer's YES

Max turned the key that was attached to the teeth. The mouth swung open and a red wooden tongue emerged. He peered inside. How could a toy eat a piece of paper? It was a silly idea. But the Wish Eater *was* really cool. He'd never seen anything like it.

"Did you find something?"

Max turned and saw his mother. He held up the Wish Eater. "This," he said.

His mother made a face. "It's kind of ugly," she said. "But you've been really patient, so if you want it, it can be your reward for helping me run all these errands."

The two of them went to the counter, where Max set the Wish Eater down.

"An excellent choice," the man said as he wrapped the Wish Eater in tissue paper and placed it inside a bag. He handed the bag to Max. "May all your wishes come true."

When Max and his mother got back to the house, the place was in an uproar. Max's older twin sisters, Elfie and Elsie, had just gotten home from softball practice and had made a mess of the kitchen, fixing themselves peanut butter and marshmallow sandwiches. His next-youngest brother, eight-year-old Charlie, had decided to paint a portrait of Aunt Maxine for her birthday and had gotten as much paint on the living room carpet as he had on the painting. And Max's youngest brother, Arthur, only three years old, was running through the house with no clothes on, laughing and banging on a pot with a wooden spoon.

"Sam!" Max's mother shouted up the stairs.

Max's father poked his head around the corner. "I'm on a call," he said, holding up his phone.

"You were supposed to be watching Arthur."

"I told Charlie to do it," Max's father said. "It's only five minutes. What can happen in five minutes?"

He disappeared back into his office while

Max's mother groaned. "A lot," she said. "Okay. Max, you take Arthur upstairs and get him dressed. I have a million things to do for the party."

"But I was going to—"

"Max, please," his mother said. "Just do it."

Max groaned. "I hate being the middle child," he said as he grabbed Arthur, who giggled and banged loudly on the pot.

It only got worse from there. At dinner, Charlie was telling a story and knocked his glass of milk over, right into Max's lap. Aunt Maxine pinched his cheeks twice. And after they cut the cake, Max left his piece on the table for a second while he went to get a fork, but Aunt Maxine's dog jumped up and ate it, so he got none.

Later, in his room, with Charlie snoring in the other bed, Max finally took the Wish Eater out of its bag. He held it in his hands. "I really wish I was an only child," he said aloud.

He thought about it. Was that really his wish? Even if it was, how could it possibly come true?

"It's all just for fun anyway," he told himself as he scrounged in his bedside table drawer for a scrap of paper and a pencil. Then he wrote his wish down, folded the paper up, and stuck it inside the Wish Eater's mouth. He placed the teeth on his bedside table and turned out the light.

When he woke up, the first thing he noticed was how quiet it was. Normally on Saturday mornings the house was filled with the sounds of his brothers and sisters. But there was nothing. He looked over at Charlie's bed. It was empty. Not only that, but it looked as if it had never been slept in.

Then he noticed the Wish Eater. He'd forgotten about it during the night. Now he opened its mouth and peered inside. His wish was gone. He poked around with his finger, thinking it must have fallen inside somehow, but there was no hole at the back of the mouth. It had simply vanished. Or been eaten. But that was impossible.

He got out of bed and went downstairs, fully expecting to find Charlie watching cartoons and the twins eating their third or fourth bowls of Krinkle-Os and arguing about whether to go skateboarding or swimming. Instead, he found only his mother and father in the kitchen. His mother was sitting at the table, drinking a cup of coffee and looking at the paper. His father was making pancakes.

"Hi, champ," his father said. "You ready for some breakfast?"

"Since when do you cook?" Max asked.

His father laughed. "Every Saturday," he said. "You know that. You want chocolate chips in yours?"

"Okay," Max said, still unsure what was happening. He sat down across from his mother. "Where is everybody?"

"Everybody who?" his mother asked.

"The others," said Max. "Charlie. Arthur. Elfie and Elsie."

"Who are they, honey?" said his mother. "New neighbors? I don't think you've mentioned them before."

Max stared at her. Was she kidding? Had

Charlie found the note he'd left inside the Wish Eater and they'd decided to play a joke on him?

His father brought over a plate of pancakes and set it down in front of Max. "Here you go, sport."

"Thanks," Max mumbled. He picked up a fork and cut off a piece of pancake. He put it in his mouth and chewed. "These are great," he said.

"You sound surprised," his father said, laughing. "You always like my pancakes. They're the best in the whole county."

Max's mother looked at him. "Are you feeling okay?" she asked.

Max nodded. He didn't mention that his father had never once made pancakes before.

"So, who were you talking about earlier?" his mother said. "All those people you wanted to know about? Elfie and Elsie? Those are funny names."

Max hesitated. He didn't know what was going on. If they weren't playing a joke on him, was he dreaming? Or had the Wish Eater really granted his wish and he was now an only child? That was ridiculous, of course. But if it *had* granted the wish, where were his brothers and sisters now? If his family was teasing him, he decided, he could play that game too.

"Nobody," he told his mother. "I was just joking around."

"What do you say we go see the new Mutant Marauders movie this afternoon," his father said. "Does that sound like fun?"

"Just us?" said Max. "Nobody else?"

"You can invite a friend if you want to," his father said. "Otherwise, yeah, just us."

Charlie had been begging their father to take them to the Mutant Marauders movie all week. There was no way he would let them go without him. Something was definitely up.

"Great," Max said. "If you're *sure* there's nobody else who should come with us."

His father laughed. "Well, your mother can come if she wants to."

"Mutant Marauders?" Max's mother said. "I think I'll let you boys see that one on your own."

"Looks like it's just the two of us," said Max's father.

Max finished his pancakes, and went to get ready for the movie. He walked through the house, looking for any signs of his brothers and sisters. There were none. No toys. No clothes. Even the photos hanging on the wall showed only Max and his parents.

It was as if Elsie, Elfie, Charlie, and Arthur had never existed.

On the drive to the movie theater, Max tried to trick his dad into admitting that the whole family was playing an elaborate joke on him.

"Don't Elsie and Elfie have a game this afternoon?" he mentioned as they drove past the softball field.

"Elsie and Elfie?" his father said, laughing. "My great-great-grandmother and her sister? I don't think they're in any shape to be playing softball. You know, since they're dead and all."

Max pretended to laugh too, as if he'd been making a joke. It was true that his sisters were named after his dad's relatives, but it was a little weird how he could so easily pretend that his own daughters didn't even exist. Part of Max was impressed by how committed he was to the joke, but another part started to feel uneasy about the whole thing.

He forgot about it during the movie, which was as awesome as he'd hoped it would be. But on the way out of the theater, he said, "We'll have to come again with Charlie. He'll love it," and his father replied, "The kid you mentioned this morning? Sure. I'll talk to his parents and make sure it's okay with them, though." Then Max felt the knot of worry in his stomach again.

He wanted to tell his dad to stop, that it

wasn't funny anymore. But he didn't want to look like he couldn't take a joke. He decided to wait and see what happened when they got home. Maybe while they were gone, his mother and siblings had put things back to normal. He bet that when he and his father walked in, everyone would be standing there with big grins on their faces, and the pictures of the whole family would be back where they belonged. Then he would laugh too, and they would all have spaghetti for dinner together like they always did on Saturday nights. He wouldn't even mind if Arthur wanted to bang on a pot with a wooden spoon.

But when they got home and opened the door, the house was still quiet. The photos on the walls still showed only Max and his parents. There was no one watching TV, or making a mess in the kitchen, or listening to music that Max didn't like. Instead, there was just his mother, sitting on the couch reading a magazine.

"How was the movie?" she asked.

"Great," Max said. He sniffed the air, expecting to smell the scent of simmering sauce.

"Are you getting a cold?" his mother asked.

Max shook his head. "I was just wondering what's for dinner," he said. "It's spaghetti night."

"Spaghetti?" his mother said. "I guess that would be different. But I thought we'd order sushi, like usual."

"Sushi?" said Max.

"You don't call it Sushi Saturday for nothing," his father said, looking at him with a puzzled expression. "Are you sure you're not coming down with something?"

"Sushi's fine," Max muttered as he walked to the stairs.

Up in his room, Max stared at the Wish Eater. It wasn't magic. It was just a toy. And yet, he was suddenly afraid of it.

He went to the dresser that he shared with Charlie. He pulled open the drawer that held their T-shirts, his on the left side and Charlie's on the right. But now the drawer was filled with only *his* shirts. Charlie's were gone.

He tugged open the other drawers. It was the same in each one. Max's clothes were folded neatly inside, but where Charlie's clothes should have been were just more in Max's size. Next, Max looked at the shelf that held their collections of books and toys. All of Max's favorites were there. But the things Charlie loved—the

Danger Squad comics, the Bear Baxter adventure novels, the Action Guy figure—they were nowhere to be seen.

"Great job, guys!" Max called out, surprising himself. "But I know you're up here."

Nobody answered him. He got down and looked under Charlie's bed, hoping to see his brother hiding there, his hand over his mouth to cover the sound of his giggling. But there was nothing. Max went and yanked open the closet door, ready to act like he knew all along that they were playing a joke on him when Charlie popped out to yell "Gotcha!"

But the closet was empty too. And only Max's clothes were hanging up inside.

Max ran into the hall, opening the nearest door. Behind it he should have found Elfie and Elsie's room. Instead, there was what looked like a home office. No posters on the walls. No clothes and sporting equipment all over the floor. No twins yelling at him to get out.

"This isn't funny anymore," Max said as he checked Arthur's room and found a generic-looking guest room instead of his baby brother's nursery. He shut the door and ran down the stairs. His parents, still in the living room, looked at him, startled.

"What's with all the yelling?" his father asked.

"You can stop pretending," Max said. "I'm sorry I wrote the wish about wanting to be an only child. I was just angry."

His parents looked at each other. For a moment, Max felt his hopes rise. Any second now they would turn to him and tell him that everything was okay, that they had only been trying to teach him a lesson about appreciating his family. And he had learned his lesson. He did appreciate them. Now he needed them to tell him the game was over.

But when they looked back at him, their expressions were ones of worry. "I really think you might be coming down with a fever," his mother said, standing up and walking over to him. She placed her hand on his forehead.

Max swatted it away. "I don't have a fever!" he said. "Now stop pretending! Go back to being like you were before."

"Before?" his father said. "Before what?"

"Before I—" Max started. Then he stopped. *Before I made my wish*, he thought to himself. And that gave him an idea. "Nothing," he said. "I guess I don't feel so great. I'm going to go lie down."

He went back to his room. Going to his desk, he took out a pen and paper and wrote out a new wish: **I WISH I HAD NEVER BOUGHT THE WISH EATER**. He folded the paper up, then picked up the Wish Eater. Turning the key to open its mouth, he placed the paper on the wooden tongue and closed the mouth again. Then he set the Wish Eater on his bedside table.

It was too early to go to bed, so he tried to distract himself by reading comic books. But every minute or two he found himself glancing over at the Wish Eater, as if maybe he could catch it in the act of chewing up his wish and swallowing it. Every time, though, it was just sitting there, unmoving.

It's not alive, he reminded himself. *It's just a*

piece of wood.

Except that wasn't true. If the Wish Eater *was* just a piece of wood or whatever, his wish would have never come true. But it had. Which meant that the Wish Eater really was magic. And that made Max very nervous.

A little while later, his mother brought him some dinner. Fortunately, it was a peanut butter and jelly sandwich, and not sushi. Max ate it, staring at the Wish Eater the whole time, imagining the sandwich was his wish. He hoped the Wish Eater would eat too and that in the morning its mouth would be empty.

Finally, it was late enough to go to bed. Max was so anxious about what would happen with his wish that he was afraid he wouldn't be able to fall asleep. He lay in the dark, wondering if the Wish Eater was silently chewing, or when it would decide whether or not to eat his wish. A couple times he almost turned the light on to check, but he worried that it might keep the magic from happening.

Eventually, he could no longer keep his eyes open and fell asleep. When he woke up, the first thing he did was look for the Wish Eater.

It was gone.

3

Max jumped out of bed. He looked all around the nightstand, in case the Wish Eater had somehow gotten knocked off it during the night. It was nowhere to be found. His heart beating excitedly, he ran out of his room and down the stairs, not caring if he woke anyone up. In fact, he hoped he did wake everyone up, because he suddenly couldn't wait to see his brothers and sisters again. He dashed into the kitchen.

"Good morning!" he said cheerfully. "What's for—"

He stopped in his tracks. The kitchen was totally empty. There were no Elfie and Elsie bickering over which one of them was the better pitcher. No Charlie spilling his orange juice. No Arthur refusing to eat his scrambled eggs unless someone made the choo-choo sound and pretended the fork was a train and his mouth was a tunnel. No anything.

Max turned around and went back upstairs. This time, he noticed that the photos on the wall were the same ones that were there yesterday, showing just him and his parents. He also noticed that all the bedrooms were still empty, and that the other bed in his room was still made up as if nobody had slept in it in a long,

long time. He didn't have to open the dresser drawers to know that they still held only his things.

He looked at the spot on his bedside table where the Wish Eater had been sitting the night before. Obviously, it had eaten his wish and granted it. It was like he had never bought it. But the Wish Eater hadn't changed everything back to how it was before.

It wasn't fair. If he had never bought the Wish Eater, then the wish he'd made should never have been granted.

Unless, of course, the Wish Eater hadn't granted his wish. Maybe it hadn't disappeared after all. Maybe someone had taken it.

He hurried down the hall to his parents' bedroom. They were just getting up.

"Did you take anything out of my room last

night?" he asked.

"Take anything?" his mother repeated. "Just your dirty socks, to put in the laundry. Why?"

"Nothing else?" Max said. "You're sure?"

"Is something missing?" his father asked.

"A toy," Max said. "A set of, um, teeth. It was sitting on my bedside table."

His father and mother both shook their heads.

Max sighed. "It's the toy I got at the store the other day," he said to his mother. "You remember it, right?"

His mother shook her head. "We didn't get anything but the vase for Aunt Maxine," she said.

"Not at the Gingerbread House," Max said. "At the other store. Frightville." Surely, he thought, his mother would remember the store filled with strange things.

"I think I'd remember a store with a name like that," his mother said. "Are you sure you didn't maybe dream about it?"

Max was about to argue with her that they had gone to Frightville, and that she had bought him the Wish Eater. Then he remembered—if his wish really had come true, and he had never bought the Wish Eater, then she couldn't remember it because it had never happened.

"Maybe," he said. "I mean, yeah, that must be it. I think I saw this thing in the window and wanted to go in, but we didn't."

"Tell you what," his father said. "Why don't we go over there today and have a look around? Maybe that thing you saw will still be there."

Max nodded. That was actually exactly what he wanted to do, to see if the Wish Eater was still on the shelf at Frightville. Now he didn't have to figure out a way to get there.

"I'll be down in a minute to make breakfast," his mother said, putting on her bathrobe. "We can go over after that, okay?"

"Thanks," Max said, leaving their bedroom and walking back to his own room. Just to make sure, he checked once again for the Wish Eater, finding nothing. It made sense to him that if he had never bought it, his mother wouldn't remember going into the store and buying it for him. But why did *he* remember it? If she had forgotten all about it, shouldn't he have forgotten too?

He couldn't wait to get to Frightville and get some answers. He hurried through breakfast, wolfing down his eggs and bacon so quickly that his parents were barely done with their coffee before he was pulling on his jacket, ready to go. He waited impatiently for them to finish, then practically dragged them to the car.

"This must be some toy," his father joked as they drove.

"There's only one of them," Max said. "I don't want anyone else to get it."

When they reached the store, he was out of the car and inside in a flash. He went to the cupboard where he'd found the Wish Eater. It wasn't there. He ran back to the front desk, where the same peculiar man from the day before was standing, polishing a snow globe that contained a miniature village.

"Hi," Max said. "Do you remember me?"

The man paused and looked at Max. He

squinted. "You do bear a resemblance to the viscount of Lower Dogsbreath," he said. "But he died in seventeen sixty-two, so I suspect you're not him. Are you a descendant?"

"Not that I know of," Max said. "I was in here the other day. I bought . . . I mean, I was looking at a toy. A set of teeth with a key that opens them. It was called the Wish Eater."

The man nodded. "Of course," he said. "A most unusual object. Only one like it I've ever come across."

"Right," Max said. "So, it's not here now."

"Alas, no," the man said. "Someone bought it."

Yes, Max wanted to say. *Me.*

"Do you remember who bought it?" he asked instead.

"I do," the man replied. "A young lady. About your age, I would think. I believe her mother called her Tamyra."

"Tamyra Hinkle?" Max asked, naming a girl in his school. He and Tamyra had been in the same English class the previous year and had worked on a project together.

"I didn't get her last name," the man said. "She had lovely curly black hair and eyes the color of chestnuts, if that helps."

"Actually, it does," Max said, as the description matched Tamyra Hinkle exactly. "Thanks."

"If you're looking for something unique, I have many more things here," the man said. He held up the snow globe and shook it. "This, for instance, commemorates the blizzard of eighteen fifty-seven, which surrounded the village of Haven by the Lake. It lasted all night, and when it was over the entire town had vanished and the only thing remaining was a rock with this globe standing on it."

"I'm good," Max said, eyeing the snow globe warily. "But thank you."

He found his parents, who were examining the items on the store shelves. "Okay," he said. "We can go."

"Did you find what you were looking for?" his father asked.

"Someone else bought it," Max said.

"Why don't you get something else?" his mother suggested. She picked up a small portrait of a woman whose eyes seemed to stare right at Max, even when he moved away. "I was thinking this might look nice in the downstairs powder room."

"I think a painting of flowers would be nicer," Max suggested.

His mother put the painting down, and

Max hurried her and his father out of the store. He had an uneasy feeling about the items in Frightville and didn't want to risk his parents buying something that would cause even more trouble than the Wish Eater had.

Also, he very much wanted to talk to Tamyra Hinkle.

4

He had to wait until lunchtime at school the next day to talk to Tamyra.

Normally, Tamyra sat at one of the corner tables where the quieter kids congregated, reading books or doing homework while they ate. Max had often seen her there, absorbed in a Harry Potter novel or working on a school project with one of her friends. Today, though, Tamyra was seated at one of the center tables where the popular kids sat. She was surrounded by a group of boisterous girls, all of them talking loudly and laughing.

"I just *love* your sweater," one of the girls said. "Where did you get it? I want one just like it."

"Um, at the Wallard's superstore," Tamyra said, pulling at the sleeve of her perfectly unremarkable blue cardigan.

The girls oohed and aahed as if it was expensive cashmere and not ordinary cotton. "We should all go there after school and get matching ones," one of them suggested, the others nodding their heads in agreement.

Max waved, trying to get Tamyra's attention. "Hey."

The girls all turned and looked at him, frowning.

"What do *you* want?" one of them asked.

"I need to talk to Tamyra," Max said. "About a, um, science assignment."

"Can't you see she's busy talking to *us*?" another girl said.

"It will just take a minute," Max assured her.

"She doesn't have a minute," said yet another girl. "We're planning Kayla's birthday party, and we need her to pick the theme. She has the *best* ideas."

Tamyra looked at Max and shrugged as her friends all started talking at once, making it impossible for him to be heard over their voices. "Maybe later," he muttered and went to sit down a few tables away.

Max watched Tamyra as he chewed on the peanut butter and banana sandwich his father had packed for him. The other girls were treating her like she was the star of the show, laughing at everything she said. Tamyra seemed to be enjoying the attention too.

But there was something strange about it. Tamyra wasn't an unpopular person, but she was definitely not the kind of girl that this group usually paid attention to. Her clothes weren't stylish. She didn't go to their parties or hang out with them after school. Now, though, it was as if something had changed overnight.

For the rest of the day, every time he saw Tamyra, she was surrounded by a group of girls. At first, she always seemed happy about this. But Max noticed that as the day went on, her expression began to grow less enthusiastic. By the time the last bell rang and everyone started to leave school for home, she was walking with her head down, an annoyed look on her face.

Half a dozen girls followed her as she made her way down the sidewalk, and although Tamyra was obviously walking quickly to get away from them, they trotted behind her.

Max caught up with them, elbowing his way through the gaggle of girls and keeping pace with Tamyra.

"I need to talk to you," he said. "It's important."

"Tay!" one of the girls behind them called out. "Should we go to Kimber's house to listen to the new Kandi Pop album, or go to Skylar's house and try on outfits for the dance?"

"I have homework to do," Tamyra shouted back.

"Okay," the girl said. "We'll go to your house and do homework."

Tamyra stopped and turned around. "You

guys go to Kimber's house," she said. "Or to Skylar's house. I don't care. But I have to do my homework *alone*."

The girls looked disappointed. One of them started to sniffle.

"Okay, fine. I'll come over to Kimber's house when I'm done," Tamyra said.

"Promise?" the girls asked in unison.

"Promise."

"Good," said one of the girls. "Then you can tell us all about your skin-care regimen. Your cheeks are practically *glowing*."

The girls split off, heading in the direction of Kimber's house and leaving Max and Tamyra by themselves.

"Tay?" Max said.

Tamyra rolled her eyes. "It's their nickname for me," she said. "So, you wanted to ask me about the science assignment?"

"Actually, no," Max replied. "I wanted to ask you about the thing you bought at Frightville yesterday."

Tamyra got a weird look on her face. "I don't know what you're talking about."

"Are you sure?" said Max. "A set of teeth? With a key that opens them?"

Tamyra shrugged. "Who says I bought something like that?"

Max wasn't sure how much to tell her about his own experience with the Wish Eater. "I was thinking about buying it. But when I went in yesterday it was gone. The man in the store told me a girl named Tamyra bought it."

Tamyra sighed. "Okay, I did," she said. "My cousin Lulu and I stopped in there, and I thought it was cool." Something in her voice sounded like she regretted what she'd done. "Anyway, I kind of wish you'd bought it before I did," she said.

"That's the thing," Max said. "I did."

Tamyra looked surprised. "So, you bought it and returned it?"

Max shook his head. Now that he'd begun the conversation, he wasn't sure how to tell Tamyra what had happened. He knew it would sound crazy. "Did you make a wish?" he asked.

"Did you?" Tamyra countered.

"Yeah," Max admitted. "I did."

"What did you wish for?"

Max took a deep breath. "I wished I was an only child. And when I woke up, I was."

Tamyra gasped.

"I don't have any brothers or sisters anymore,"

Max continued. "It's like they never existed."

"That's impossible," Tamyra said. "People don't just disappear. And I've never even heard you mention brothers or sisters."

"You've met them," Max said. "My sisters, Elfie and Elsie, are twins. Your softball team played against theirs last year. Elsie struck you out."

Tamyra shook her head again. "I don't remember them at all. Sorry."

"It's the Wish Eater," Max said. "It made it so they never existed. My brothers too. I'm the only one who remembers them."

"That's—"

"Impossible," Max said before she could. "You mentioned that already."

"Well, it is," Tamyra said.

Max knew arguing with her wasn't going

to help. "What did you wish for?" he asked instead. "Did it have anything to do with how all those girls are suddenly your best friends?"

Tamyra was silent. She obviously didn't want to talk about it, but Max needed to know. He stood with his arms crossed, waiting for her to tell him everything.

"This is ridiculous," Tamyra said. "That thing isn't magic. You're just sorry you returned it. Now you want me to give it to you, so you made up that crazy story about your sisters and brothers disappearing to make me feel sorry for you."

She turned and walked away. Max wondered if he should chase after her. He decided not to. Tamyra wasn't ready to talk yet. He hoped she would be soon, though. He didn't know how he was going to get the Wish Eater to reverse his wish, but he couldn't even try if he didn't have it to work with.

For now, all he could do was go home and wait.

5

When Max got home, the house was empty.

He went upstairs, trying not to think about Elfie, Elsie, Charlie, and Arthur. But they were all he *could* think about. As he sat at his desk, trying to focus on the book report he was supposed to be writing for Mrs. Heneka's class, he pictured his brothers and sisters in his mind. He tried to remember exactly what they looked like and how their voices sounded.

He thought Charlie had a scar on his chin, from the time they were playing tag at the beach and he'd slipped in the sand and cut himself on a shell. But maybe the scar was on his forehead and had been caused by running into an open cupboard door. Now Max wasn't positive.

It was like even his memories of them were disappearing. Max took out his phone and opened the photo app. He knew he'd taken a couple shots of his brothers and sisters at Aunt Maxine's birthday party. But when he scrolled through the images on his phone, none of those pictures were there. Only ones with his parents remained.

He set the phone down and pulled open his desk drawer, looking for the school yearbook. When he found it, he flipped it open and turned to the section with photos of the sports teams. The one of the softball team showed a lot of faces he recognized, but Elfie and Elsie weren't among them. In the group photos, he looked up his fifth-grade class. There he was, standing in between Dax Luftig and Karice Simpson. But the photo of the second-grade class was missing Charlie.

He shoved the yearbook back into the drawer, slamming it closed. Getting up, he ran to Elfie and Elsie's bedroom and went inside. Everything that made the room theirs was gone: the sports equipment that was always piled in the corner, the clothes that littered the floor, the posters of Serena Williams and Lindsey Vonn. The boring office furniture that had replaced it looked lifeless and cold.

On the desk was a framed photo of Max with his parents. He was in the middle, and they were all smiling. Max turned it facedown on the desk and left the room. Being alone in the house was reminding him how much he missed the noise and chaos his siblings caused, even though it sometimes made him crazy. Right now, he would even be happy to be giving Arthur a bath.

He stood in the hallway and closed his eyes, trying again to picture the faces of his brothers and sisters. This time, he could see only ghostly images of them. Even those started to fade after a few seconds.

Max ran into his room and found a pad of paper. He wrote **Elfie** at the top, then stopped. He knew he had another sister. What was her name?

"Elsie," he said finally, scribbling it down before he could forget again. Then he added **Charlie** and **Archie** beneath that. He looked at the list. Were all the names right? He didn't think they were.

He went over to his bookshelf and pulled out his well-loved copy of *Green Eggs and Ham*. Turning to the inside, he looked for the names he knew should be written there. The book had been given to Elfie and Elsie by Aunt Maxine. Then it had been handed down to Max, then Charlie. Only recently, Charlie had decided that it was time for their baby brother to have it, even though he couldn't read it himself yet. Charlie had written the new name in just like Max had written Charlie's name in it when he'd given it to him.

Max expected the page to be blank, or to show only his name, and was almost afraid to look at it. But there on the paper was the list of names. It was as if the Wish Eater's magic had overlooked this one little bit of proof that he hadn't made up his brothers and sisters. And even as Max read the list of names, they began to fade.

"Arthur," he said as the letters, written in Charlie's crooked printing, melted into nothing. "Not Archie. Arthur."

He quickly wrote the name on the pad, crossing out Archie and putting Arthur in its place. Then he read the list out loud: "Elfie. Elsie. Charlie. Arthur." Now that they were written down, he wouldn't forget them. He folded the paper and tucked it into his shirt pocket, where it rested against his heart.

For the rest of the night, whenever he felt himself forgetting his brothers and sisters, he touched the paper in his pocket. He did it twice at dinner and several more times while doing his homework. Before he went to bed, he took the paper out and read the names again.

"I'm not going to forget you," he promised. "I'm going to get you back."

He meant what he said. The problem was, he had no idea how he was going to do it. After turning the light off, he lay in bed, thinking about the Wish Eater and how he'd messed up his wish. If he ever got the chance to use it again, he was going to have to make sure he did it correctly. But that meant getting Tamyra to let him have it back, and given how she'd acted that afternoon, she wasn't ready to do that.

Max stayed awake for a long time, and when he finally fell asleep it seemed like only a few minutes before his alarm rang and he had to get up and get ready. So when he walked into school, he was yawning and at first didn't notice the huge crowd that was blocking the hallway.

"Tay is *my* best friend!" a girl said, sounding angry.

"She was my best friend first," said another.

Suddenly, a lot of people were talking at once, all of them insisting that Tamyra was *their* best friend. Max searched and found Tamyra standing in the center of the arguing students, looking miserable. When she saw Max, she pushed her way through the throng.

"Come on," she said. "I need your help."

Max followed her as she hurried down the corridor. Behind them, the kids arguing about which of them was Tamyra's best friend noticed that she was gone.

"There she is!" one of them shouted. "Hey, Tay, wait up."

Tamyra began to run. Max, seeing a bunch of people running toward them, ran too. Tamyra turned a corner ahead of him, disappearing. When Max reached the corner, she was gone. Then a door opened and a hand reached out, pulling him inside a closet where janitorial supplies were kept. Tamyra shut the door behind him. A second later, the sound of running feet and voices filled the hallway.

"Shhh," Tamyra whispered, holding her finger to her lips.

Max stayed quiet until the sounds outside

stopped.

"I think they're gone," he said softly.

"Good," said Tamyra, unzipping her back-pack. She reached inside and pulled out the Wish Eater. "Because we've got some wishing to do."

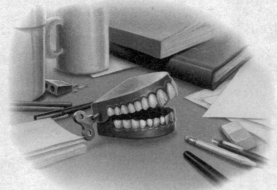

Max stared at the Wish Eater sitting on Tamyra's outstretched palm. Seeing it again, he couldn't believe that a toy could cause so much trouble.

"It doesn't look magic, does it?" he said.

"I wish I'd never seen it," said Tamyra.

After a second, they both laughed. "Probably not the best choice of words," Max said.

"Just for the record, that's not my wish," said

Tamyra.

"It only counts if you write it down," Max reminded her.

"Too bad it didn't come with a rule book," Tamyra remarked, sitting down cross-legged on the floor. "Then we might have made different wishes."

Max joined her on the floor. The Wish Eater sat between them. "I don't know if that would have helped," he said. "I think this thing is tricky."

They both stared at the teeth in silence for a moment. Then Tamyra said, "How do you think it works?"

Max shook his head. "I don't know," he said. "All I know is, it does."

"It still doesn't make any sense," Tamyra said. "Magic, I mean. Like, why is this thing magic? If I made a Wish Eater out of clay or whatever, it wouldn't be."

"Maybe it would be," Max suggested. He looked at Tamyra. "You still don't believe it's real, do you? Not really."

Tamyra shrugged. "I like science," she answered. "Things that you can explain by studying them. Magic, I'm not so sure about."

"But you love the Harry Potter books," Max said. "You wear a Ravenclaw scarf and everything."

"That's just for fun," Tamyra said. "I do love the books. And I love the *idea* of magic. But it's not real."

"Then how do you explain what's going on?" Max asked. "My family disappearing. You suddenly being the most popular girl in school."

Tamyra didn't answer him. She fidgeted uncomfortably for a moment, then said, "Who should go first, you or me?"

Max wanted to say he would, but that seemed greedy. Also, he kind of wanted to see if Tamyra's wish worked before he made his. "You go first," he said.

Tamyra seemed relieved at the suggestion. She took a notebook out of her backpack, tore off a page, then sat quietly, tapping her pen against her leg and biting her lip.

Max waited impatiently until he couldn't stand it any longer. "What are you going to wish for?"

Tamyra started to write on the paper. "I wish I wasn't the most popular girl in school anymore," she said as she wrote. "How does that sound?"

"Pretty good," Max said.

Tamyra folded up the paper. She opened the Wish Eater's mouth, tucked the note inside, then shut it again. "How long do you think it will take?" she asked.

"I left mine in overnight," Max said. "How about you?"

"Same," said Tamyra. "I hope it doesn't take that long this time." She put the Wish Eater back into her backpack and zipped it shut. "I guess I should keep it with me until something happens."

Or doesn't happen, Max thought. But he didn't say that out loud. He didn't want Tamyra to worry about it.

"We'd better get to class," Tamyra said, opening the door a crack and peering out. "It's okay," she told Max. "My fan club is gone."

They stepped out into the hall and walked toward their classrooms. Max's homeroom was first, and when they reached the door Tamyra said, "You can take the Wish Eater home tonight and make your wish."

"Okay," Max said. "Good luck with yours. I hope it comes true."

Tamyra smiled. "Me too."

Max went into his classroom just as the bell rang. He slipped into his seat and unpacked his books as the morning announcements came on.

"Today's hot lunch will be fish sticks," said the robotic voice of Mrs. Blovage, the principal's assistant. "Tryouts for the school play will be held during sixth period, and all interested thespians should report to Mr. Coney's room. And in this morning's big news, the results of yesterday's student council election are in and Tamyra Hinkle was elected to every single position. Congratulations to President-Vice-President-Treasurer-Secretary Hinkle. I'm sure you'll do an excellent job."

The class erupted in applause, and Max heard several people say that they had voted for Tamyra, who as far as Max knew hadn't even been running for student council. The Wish Eater had obviously taken her wish seriously and also apparently hadn't answered her latest one yet. Max wondered if it even would and how it decided which ones to say yes to and which ones to ignore.

He had to wait until lunch period to see Tamyra again, and he spent the whole time thinking about how he was going to word his own wish later that night. He was still thinking about it on the way to the lunchroom when his train of thought was interrupted by a loud *"Psst."*

He stopped and looked around.

"Over here," a voice whispered.

He turned and saw Tamyra waving to him from the same closet they'd hidden in earlier. He went inside.

"Are they still looking for me?" Tamyra asked.

"Who?" said Max.

"The angry mob," said Tamyra.

"What angry mob? I thought you were everybody's favorite president-vice-president-treasurer-secretary."

"I was," said Tamyra. "Until this thing decided to grant my wish." She held up the Wish Eater and opened its mouth. Her wish was gone. "Now I'm not the most popular girl in school anymore. I'm the most *un*popular."

Max thought about what Tamyra had written as her wish. "'I wish I wasn't the most popular girl in school anymore,'" he said.

"Exactly," said Tamyra. "I thought that would do it. And it did. Only it did it too well. Now everybody is saying I cheated to win the election. But I didn't even run!"

A moment later, the sound of people coming down the hall filled the closet.

"I can't believe we thought she was nice!" a girl's voice said indignantly.

"I always knew she was a phony," said another. "I hear they caught her cheating on her math test too."

Tamyra shut her eyes and groaned. "See?" she muttered.

"We can fix this," Max said. "You just have to wish again. Only this time we'll write it really carefully."

Tamyra shook her head. "I'll just make it worse," she said.

"Down with Hinkle!" a voice shouted. It was joined by many others. "Down with Hinkle! Down with Hinkle!"

"I'm not sure it could get worse," Max said. "Sorry," he added when Tamyra covered her eyes with her hand.

"Okay," Tamyra said. "One more wish. But you take this thing home with you. I don't want it anywhere near me."

She thrust the Wish Eater at Max, who took it. Despite everything, he felt a little thrill holding it in his hands again.

"What do you want to wish this time?" he

asked.

Tamyra took out some paper and a pen. She wrote something down, then folded the paper up and handed it to Max. "Here," she said. "Put it in that thing tonight."

"You're not going to tell me what it says?" Max asked.

Tamyra shook her head. "Nope. Just do it. I'll text you if it works. Assuming it eats it, that is."

Max shoved the wish into his pocket. "Now what?" he said. "You can't let those girls find you."

Tamyra clutched her stomach and groaned. "I think I've come down with the flu," she said, obviously faking it. "I'm going to see if I can go home."

Max grinned. "Is that any way for the

student body president-vice-president-treasurer-secretary to act?"

"Hopefully, tomorrow that won't be a problem," Tamyra said. "You just make sure you put that wish in, okay?"

"Like I could forget," said Max as Tamyra opened the door.

As Tamyra snuck off down the hall in the direction of the nurse's office, Max went back to his homeroom and stowed the Wish Eater in his backpack. He thought about it for the rest of the day, and when he got home that afternoon he took it out and set it on his bedside table.

He retrieved Tamyra's note from his pocket. He was tempted to open it and read it, but he thought that might be cheating, so he opened the Wish Eater's mouth and put the wish on its extended tongue. Then he sat staring at it for a while longer. He really wanted to make a wish of his own. The more he thought about it, the more he wondered why he couldn't.

"Nobody said you only had to make one wish at a time," he said to himself.

He fetched a piece of paper and a pen, then wrote out his new wish. He read it over, decided it was exactly right, and folded it up. Then he opened the Wish Eater's mouth again. The red tongue stuck out. Tamyra's wish was still sitting on it. Max placed his on top of hers, then closed the mouth.

"Let's hope we both get what we wished for," he said as he placed the Wish Eater back on his bedside table.

7

The first thing Max did the next morning was check the Wish Eater's mouth. When he saw that it was empty, his heart leaped with joy.

He looked over at Charlie's bed. It was still made up, and it didn't look slept in. But maybe, he thought, the Wish Eater had answered his wish only moments ago, and Charlie hadn't slept there. Maybe his brothers and sisters were somewhere else in the house. His heart pounding, he jumped out of bed and ran into the hallway. He dashed to the door of the twins' room and looked inside. It was still an office. Then he checked Arthur's room, but it was also unchanged.

He tried not to worry as he went downstairs, telling himself that maybe everyone was gathered in the kitchen. But the house was too quiet, and when he got to the kitchen, all he saw was his parents sitting at the table, quietly looking at the newspaper and eating bowls of oatmeal.

"Good morning," his mother said. "Do you want scrambled eggs or cereal today?"

"Um, is anyone else here?" Max asked, still hopeful.

"Just us," said his father. "Why? You expecting company?"

"I, uh, thought I heard someone," Max said. "Never mind. I'll go get dressed."

"Eggs or cereal?" his mother called after him.

"Cereal," Max grumbled as he went upstairs.

Back in his room, he pulled on his clothes, wondering what had gone wrong this time. The Wish Eater sat on his bedside table, grinning in a way that made him feel like it was laughing at him.

"I know you answered my wish," Max said to it. "But how? What did you do now?"

The Wish Eater remained annoyingly silent. Max finished getting dressed, then picked the toy up and stuffed it into his backpack. He carried the backpack downstairs with him and set it by the door before rejoining his parents. As he was eating his Oatey Bits, his phone vibrated. He looked at the screen and saw a text from

Tamyra: We have a problem.

He texted her back: ???

She replied instantly: Meet me on the corner in 5.

Max set his phone down and spooned cereal into his mouth as quickly as he could.

"What's the hurry?" his father asked.

"I've got to get to school a little early," Max said, which was kind of true and therefore not a lie.

"Big test?" asked his mother.

"Something like that," said Max, picking up his bowl and tipping the last of the milk into his mouth. He took the bowl to the sink. "Bye," he said to his parents.

"Have a good day!" they called out as he went to the front door, picked up his backpack, and left the house.

Tamyra lived three streets over. As Max walked down the sidewalk toward her street, he could see her standing on the corner. But there were three other kids standing with her whom he didn't recognize. As he got closer, he saw that one of them was a boy and the other two were girls.

"Hey," he said, waving. Tamyra didn't look happy. "Are these your cousins or something?"

"No," said Tamyra. She took a deep breath. "They're my brother and sisters."

"You don't have . . ." Max began, then stopped. He looked at the kids again. The two girls looked an awful lot alike. His mouth fell open as a horrible thought came to him.

"I do *now*," Tamyra said. "Max, meet Elfie, Elsie, and Charlie."

"Hi!" the three kids said together. They

smiled happily.

Max stared at them, speechless.

"Before you ask, Arthur is at home with my aunt Jackie," Tamyra said. "And my parents think this is all totally normal, like there have always been five kids."

Max continued to stare at the kids. "Wow," he said finally. "That's really bizarre."

"You think?" said Tamyra. "So, did you make a wish last night? That your brothers and sisters would be back?"

"Yeah," Max admitted. "I added it to yours."

Tamyra groaned. Behind her, Elsie and Elfie laughed. Max found himself stealing glances at them. The resemblance to Tamyra was obvious. The fact that they had his sisters' names was freaky.

"The Wish Eater granted your wish but

gave it to me," Tamyra said.

"Your wish was gone too," said Max. "But nothing was different at my house."

Tamyra got a funny look on her face.

"What?" Max said.

"Nothing," Tamyra said. "I mean, it's probably nothing. It's just that my wish wasn't anything to do with my family."

"What was it?" Max asked warily.

"We're going to be late for school," Charlie announced. "And I have a test."

"Let's walk," Tamyra suggested, heading off in the direction of the school. Her sisters and brother followed. Max walked beside Tamyra.

"What did you wish?" he asked her, since she hadn't really answered his question.

"Just that things would be the way they were before I wished the first time," Tamyra said.

"Oh," Max said, relieved. "That doesn't sound so bad."

Tamyra nodded but didn't say anything. When they reached the school, Elsie and Elfie headed off to the seventh-grade classrooms, while Charlie joined the other third graders, all of whom seemed to know who he was.

"This is so weird," said Tamyra. "It's like they've been going here forever."

Max started to say something, but just then Ji-woo Pak came rushing up to him, along with Amber Maitling and Pihu Reddy. They were three of the girls who had been angry at Tamyra the day before. Now they ignored her, focusing all their attention on Max.

"Congratulations!" Ji-woo said, grabbing his arm and squeezing it.

"Uh, thanks?" Max said.

"You haven't seen the list?" Pihu asked.

"List?" said Max

"The cheer squad list," said Amber, jumping up and down. "You made the team!"

"This is *so* great," Ji-woo said. "You'll be the first boy on the squad."

Max looked at the three girls. "There must be some mistake," he said. "I didn't try—"

Tamyra kicked him in the leg.

"Ow!" Max said, looking at her. "What was that for?"

"It's my wish," Tamyra hissed in his ear.

"Our first practice is this afternoon," said Pihu. "That's when you'll get your pom-poms."

"Pom-poms?" Max said.

Amber produced a pair of pom-poms in the

school colors of blue and gold. She waved them in Max's face. "Goooooo Badgers!" she shouted, then twirled around.

Ji-woo and Pihu also shrieked, "Go Badgers!" They looked expectantly at Max.

"Oh," he said. "Go Badgers?"

Pihu frowned. "More energy," she said.

"Go Badgers!" Max shouted, earning himself looks from all the kids in the hallway.

"Better," Pihu said. "I can't wait to see your herkie."

"My what?" Max asked as the three girls ran off, giggling and waving their pom-poms. He turned to Tamyra and scowled.

"I might have made one tiny little extra wish," Tamyra said.

"To be on the cheer team?" said Max.

"I figured it wouldn't hurt," Tamyra said.

"My other wishes all turned out bad, and I wanted *something* good to happen."

Max groaned.

"The good news is, no one is mad at me anymore," Tamyra said. "So that part turned out okay."

"We've got to fix this," Max said. "And fast. I can't be on the cheer squad."

"Why not?" said Tamyra, putting her hands on her hips. "Because you think it's just for girls?"

"No," Max said. "Because I'm totally uncoordinated. Haven't you ever seen me try to dance?"

"Actually, I have," said Tamyra. "At Tanner Bexler's birthday party. It wasn't pretty."

"Exactly," Max said. "And now they want to see my herkie. What even is that?"

"It's a cheer move," Tamyra said. "Where you—"

"I don't want to know!" Max interrupted. "Because I'm not doing it. We're going to fix this. All of it. We're going to get rid of your new brothers and sisters, and I'm not going to be on the cheer squad."

Tamyra looked sad.

"What?" said Max.

"It sounds so weird when you say it like that," Tamyra said. "Getting rid of my brothers and sisters. I mean, I know they're not sup- posed to be here. But they are. If we wish them away, what happens to them?"

Max thought about it. But he didn't know either. And now that Tamyra had brought it up, it did sound kind of horrible. The new Elfie, Elsie, Charlie, and Arthur were real people. At least, he thought they were.

"We'll figure it out," he said as the first bell rang and everybody rushed to get to their homerooms.

The problem was, he had no idea how.

8

"Good overhead clasp, Amber," Coach Digmore said.

She walked down the line, scrutinizing each person's form as they worked through a series of poses she'd taught them during the first part of practice. She stopped in front of Max and gave him a steely stare. "Daggers!" she barked.

Max straightened his back and brought his arms up, his elbows at his waist and his fists touching his shoulders. He waited for Coach Digmore to tell him he was doing it wrong.

"Not bad," she said, nodding approvingly. She blew the whistle that hung from a cord around her neck. "Take five," she said. "When we come back, we're doing it all with poms."

The squad gathered around Max, patting him on the back.

"You're doing great," Amber assured him.

"Thanks," Max said. "It's harder than it looks."

"Right?" Ji-woo said. "My brother and his buddies on the football team think all we do is jump around and make up cheers. He has *no* idea. Wait until they all see another guy doing what we do."

Max didn't say anything. He hoped nobody would ever see him doing this. If he finally wished correctly, and the Wish Eater granted it, it would be Tamyra on the squad and he would have his brothers and sisters back. But given how things had worked out so far, those were two big ifs. The Wish Eater seemed to play by its own rules, and the rules kept changing. He and Tamyra had arranged to meet at her house after school and sort their wishes out once and for all.

First, though, he had to make it through cheer squad practice. Coach Digmore came back, carrying a big cardboard box, which she set on the gym floor. All the girls who were new to the squad rushed over, reaching in and grabbing pairs of pom-poms.

"Come on, Max," the coach called. "Get your poms."

Max walked reluctantly over to the box and

pulled out two of the fluffy bundles of plastic strips.

"Now shake 'em!" Coach Digmore ordered.

Max lifted the pom-poms up and rustled them. Strings of plastic got in his mouth.

"They're not a snack, Max," Ji-woo joked as the others laughed.

"Okay, squad," Coach Digmore said. "Back in line. Our first game is Friday night, and we've got to be ready."

For the next hour, Max and the rest of the squad ran through their moves. By the end of practice, Max was exhausted. When the coach blew her whistle, he gratefully stuffed his pom-poms into his backpack and headed for the doors.

"Good work today, Max," the coach called after him. "We'll have you doing cupies in no time."

"Can't wait!" Max called back.

Fifteen minutes later, he was in Tamyra's bedroom.

"What's a cupie?" he asked, as he opened his backpack and took out the Wish Eater. The pom-poms came with it, landing on the floor.

Tamyra picked the pom-poms up and waved them sadly. "It's a cheer stunt where you toss a flyer into the air."

"I am not getting tossed," Max said firmly.

"Don't worry," said Tamyra. "The flyer is always the smallest person. You'll be a base."

Max raised an eyebrow.

"One of the people who tosses the flyer," Tamyra explained. She set the pom-poms on the bed and sighed. "I'd love to be a flyer."

Max held up the Wish Eater. "If we wish right, you might be," he reminded her.

"I've been thinking about that," Tamyra said. "First, I think we need to do one wish at a time. Making two wishes backfired big-time."

Max nodded in agreement. "So, which thing do we undo first?" he asked. "The extra and missing brothers and sisters, or this cheer squad business?"

Before Tamyra could answer, Charlie appeared in the doorway. He was carrying Arthur. "What are you guys doing?" he asked.

"Just something for school," Tamyra said.

"Can we play too?" Charlie asked.

"We're not playing," said Tamyra. "Why don't you go watch a video?"

"Catterbox!" Arthur exclaimed. He pointed his little hand at the Wish Eater and waved it excitedly.

"What?" Tamyra said.

"Catterbox!" Arthur said again.

"I think he means Chatterbox," said Max. "He's a dragon in a TV show. *The Enchanted Castle*. Arthur—my Arthur—loves it. Chatterbox has teeth that look like the Wish Eater's. They chatter when he's nervous, which he always is."

Arthur wriggled in Charlie's arms. Charlie set him down, and the little boy ran into the room, holding out his hands. "Catterbox!"

"This isn't a toy," Tamyra said, holding the Wish Eater out of his reach.

Arthur screwed up his face. A moment later, he began to wail. Tamyra looked at Max. "I've never had a little brother," she said. "What do we do?"

Max looked around the room. Spying the pom-poms on Tamyra's bed, he picked them up. He held them to his chest, then thrust them out and wiggled them around. "Huffle-puffle," he chanted. "Huffle-puffle. Badgers stomp and badgers snuffle."

It was one of the cheer squad's chants. Coach Digmore had handed out a sheet of them at practice, and Max had glanced over the words. Now he tried to recall them as he moved his hands into a high touchdown formation and grunted like he imagined a badger might.

Arthur stopped crying and sat down on the floor. He clapped his hands happily and laughed. Max lowered the pom-poms, and the little boy frowned.

"Do it again!" Tamyra said.

Max repeated the chant, stomping and

snuffling as he waved the pom-poms in the air. Arthur laughed so hard that he fell over. Even Charlie and Tamyra were giggling wildly by the time Max was done.

"That's so great," Tamyra said. "I can't wait to see you do that in front of the whole school."

"Well, you won't get the chance," Max said. "Unless you want to make a wish about You Know What," he added, looking meaningfully at Charlie and Arthur.

"We can do your wish first," Tamyra said. She went to her desk and took out some paper and crayons. Sitting on the floor, she gave a sheet of paper and some of the crayons to Arthur. He took a purple crayon and started scribbling on the paper. Charlie, having lost interest in what Max and Tamyra were doing, wandered off.

Max watched Arthur draw.

"This must be really weird for you," Tamyra said.

Max nodded. "For you too," he said.

Tamyra shrugged. "To tell you the truth, I'm kind of getting used to them."

"Even Elfie and Elsie?" Max asked.

Tamyra laughed. "Even them," she said.

Max took one of the sheets of paper. "What should I wish?" he asked.

"What if you say something like 'I wish my life was the way it was before I bought the Wish Eater and made my first wish'?" Tamyra suggested.

"That seems too easy," said Max.

"Do you have a better idea?"

"No," Max admitted. He wrote the wish down on the paper, then tore off the piece with the words on it and folded it up. He took the Wish Eater and placed the paper in its mouth, then set it on the floor. "Do you mind keeping this here tonight?" he asked Tamyra. "I don't want to be tempted to change my wish, or keep checking on it. Besides, if everything works out, you'll need it next anyway."

"Sure," Tamyra said. "And I have a feeling that this time it will work out."

"I hope so," Max said. "The first assembly is Friday, and I do not want the entire school to see my herkie."

9

The first thing Max noticed when he woke up was that it was pitch-dark. He thought it must still be nighttime. But he wasn't tired, and something about the darkness seemed artificial, as if the windows in his room had been covered up. Then he reached out his hand to turn on the bedside light and touched something soft. He felt around some more and realized that his bed was surrounded by velvet curtains.

He pushed the curtain closest to him aside and discovered that it was indeed morning. And although he was in a bedroom, it wasn't *his* bedroom. For one thing, this bedroom was round. Also, it was made of stone. The floor. The walls. The ceiling. All of it was made out of stone blocks. The windows were just holes in the stone walls, with no glass covering them, and a warm breeze wafted in.

Max sniffed. The air had a strange scent to it, like a burned-out match or a smoky campfire. Fearing that wherever he was might be on fire, he scrambled out of bed and ran to the window. Looking out, he gasped. He was in the tower of a castle. Spread below him was the rest of it, a sprawling pile of stones with more towers, a drawbridge, and a moat surrounding the whole thing. Beyond the castle were rolling green hills covered in flowers. A single, narrow dirt road wound through the hills to the front gate.

As he looked out the window, a huge shadow passed overhead, accompanied by another whiff of the peculiar smell. Max looked up and gasped again as a fat dragon with purple-and-blue scales swooped lazily over the top of the tower. It belched loudly, puffing out a stream of smoke.

"Chatterbox!" Max exclaimed.

He couldn't believe it. The dragon from the TV show was flying around outside his window. And that could mean only one thing.

"We're in the Enchanted Castle," said a voice behind him.

He turned to see Charlie standing there. *His* Charlie. Not Tamyra's Charlie. Max ran to his brother and gave him a big hug.

"Hey!" Charlie said. "What's the big deal?"

"You're back!" said Max.

"What do you mean back?" said Charlie, looking bewildered. "You just saw me last night when we went to bed."

"But," Max began. "Wait. You mean you've just been asleep this whole time?"

Charlie nodded. "I went to bed, and when I woke up, I was here. Where did you think I was?"

Max's brain was racing. He still had no idea how the Wish Eater's magic worked, but if what Charlie was saying was true, his brothers and sisters didn't even know that they'd disappeared and been gone for almost a week.

"What I want to know is, how did we get here?" Charlie said, going to the window and looking out. "Is this, like, some kind of theme park? And how did we get here without waking up?"

"Have you seen the others?" Max asked him. "Elfie, Elsie, and Arthur?"

Charlie shook his head. "Wow," he said. "That Chatterbox robot looks so real."

"Come on," Max said, going over and taking him by the hand. "We've got to find everybody else."

He dragged Charlie out of the room and into a narrow corridor. They walked past a door to another bedroom (Max assumed this was where Charlie had woken up) and found themselves at the top of a staircase that spiraled down. Descending to the next level, they found two more bedrooms. They also found Elfie, Elsie, and Arthur.

"What's going on?" Elfie asked when she saw her brothers. "Where are Mom and Dad?"

"Um, at breakfast, I think," Max said, resisting the urge to hug them like he had Charlie.

Just then, Tamyra appeared, coming up the staircase from the next level. With her were the other Elfie, Elsie, Charlie, and Arthur. When they saw Max's family, they stopped, all of them staring at one another.

"You look like us," Max's Charlie said.

"You look like *us*," said Tamyra's Charlie.

The two Elfies and two Elsies said nothing, but they stared at one another for a moment longer before saying "Cool!" all together, then giving each other high fives.

"We've never met other twins our age," the two Elsies said simultaneously, then high-fived again.

The two Arthurs pointed to the window in the tower wall. "Catterbox!" they said.

Chatterbox the dragon was, in fact, hovering outside the tower, peering in at them with one big golden eye. His giant teeth started to chatter, clacking together nervously. Looking at them, Max was reminded of the Wish Eater.

"I think I know what happened," he said. "Arthur—your Arthur—was drawing a picture while we were talking. I remember seeing him draw something that looked like Chatterbox."

"Right," Tamyra said. "And then he drew some people."

"Elfie, Elsie, Charlie, and you," Max said. "The whole family."

"But how did that get us here?" Tamyra asked.

Max went over to Tamyra's Arthur. "Arthur," he said. "Did you do something with the picture you drew?"

Arthur laughed. "Fed it!" he said. "To Catterbox!"

Max turned to Tamyra. "He must have seen us put our wish inside the Wish Eater's mouth. When we weren't looking, he did the same thing with his picture."

"Of course," Tamyra said. "And the Wish Eater granted both wishes again. You got your brothers and sisters back, and Arthur brought all of us to meet Chatterbox."

"What are you two talking about?" Max's Elsie asked.

"Yeah," said Tamyra's Elsie. "What's all this about wishes?"

"It's a long story," Max told them. "And you

probably wouldn't believe it anyway. The important thing is, how are we going to get out of here and back home?"

"Can't Mom and Dad just drive us?" Max's Elfie asked.

"Uh, it's not that simple," said Max. "Like I said, it's a long story."

"With!" the two Arthurs said. "Make a with!"

Max looked at Tamyra. "I don't suppose the Wish Eater came along with you?"

"Nope," Tamyra said. "As usual, it made up its own rules and sent us away. It's probably still sitting on my desk back home."

Max sighed. He looked out the window, where Chatterbox had given up spying on them and flown off. They were stuck inside a tower in the Enchanted Castle. "I don't imagine any-one knows any spells to get us out of here," he said.

"Wandsworth," his Charlie said.

"Who?" said Max.

"Wandsworth the Worst," said Tamyra's Charlie. "He's the wizard who lives in the Enchanted Castle."

"Why is he the worst?" Tamyra asked.

"Because his spells mostly don't work right," her Charlie explained.

"Kind of like our wishes," Tamyra said. "Well, unless someone has a better idea, I say we find this Wandsworth and see if he can help us. Where is he?"

The two Charlies looked at each other and grinned. "In the Dreary Dungeon."

The Dreary Dungeon really was dreary. Located far beneath the Enchanted Castle, it was reached by a series of stone staircases below the kitchen. The stones were covered in slimy green moss, which was fed by water that dripped continuously from the low ceiling. The air grew colder and damper the deeper Max, Tamyra, and the others went, and even the lighted torches that were stuck into iron holders at regular intervals couldn't make the place seem more cheerful. The two Elfies carried the two Arthurs, and the two Charlies led the way, since they were the ones who watched the TV show the most and knew where they were going.

Finally, they reached the bottom of the stairs and found themselves at a big wooden door. An iron knocker in the shape of a dragon's head was in the center of the door. Max took hold of the ring the dragon held in its mouth and rapped it three times.

"What do you want?" a creaky voice shouted, sounding irritated.

"That's Wandsworth," the Charlies said. "He's always in a bad mood."

A moment later, the door opened a crack, and a long nose poked out at about the height of Max's belly button. This was followed by a bushy gray mustache, then an unruly beard that dragged on the floor. A huge spider crawled out of the beard, followed by two more, then all three disappeared back into the bushy gray tangle of hair as, finally, the face that the nose and beard belonged to emerged and a pair of dark eyes glared at the group of kids.

"How did you get in here?" Wandsworth asked. "I distinctly recall putting the drawbridge up. Those door-to-door potion salesmen have been particularly pestering of late."

"We, um, kind of wished ourselves here," Max explained.

Wandsworth's eyebrows knitted together in a scowl. "Wished?" he growled.

"Well, Arthur did," Max elaborated, pointing to Tamyra's brother.

"Is he a wizard?" asked Wandsworth.

"Oh no," said Max. "At least, I don't think he is. He's only three."

"When I was three, I turned my nanny into a goat," Wandsworth said. "Can't he even do that?"

"None of us are wizards," said Tamyra. "This is all because of the Wish Eater."

"Fish eater?" Wandsworth said. "Don't care much for it myself. Prefer mutton."

"*Wish* Eater," Max said. "It's a thing you feed wishes to. It looks like a set of teeth."

"A set of dragon teeth," Tamyra added. "Well, small ones, anyway."

"Dragon teeth, you say?" Wandsworth said.

"Is that important?" Max asked.

"Chatterbox has a brother," Wandsworth said. "His name is Gabblejaw. He belongs to a rival wizard. My brother, actually. I heard he turned some of Gabblejaw's baby teeth into a magical item. Your Wish Eater may be it. If so, that explains it. Dragon magic is unpredictable."

"Right," Max said, as if everyone knew this. "Anyway, we were hoping you might be able to help us get back home."

"And maybe sort out some other problems," Tamyra added.

"Why would I do that?" Wandsworth asked.

Max looked at Tamyra. "Um, because you're a wizard?"

Wandsworth snorted. "Can't you ask the eater of wishes to do it?"

"We don't exactly have it right now," Max told him. "It brought us here, but it stayed behind."

Wandsworth glowered at them. He was

clearly annoyed at being interrupted at whatever it was he was doing.

"Or if you're busy, maybe we can ask your
brother for help," Max suggested.

"You might—if I hadn't gotten into an
argument with him and turned him into a
toad," said Wandsworth, regarding them with
an expression suggesting he was thinking of
doing the same to all of them.

"Pwease?" the two Arthurs said.

Wandsworth sighed. "Well, if it's the only
way to get rid of you all, I *might* be able to help
you. It depends on what kind of mood he's in
today."

"He?" Tamyra said.

"Chatterbox," the wizard said, stepping
through the door and shutting it behind him.
"Come on. We'll see what we can do."

He began the long trudge up the stairs, the kids forming a line behind him. His legs were very short, and it took a long time, but eventually they reached the kitchen again. Wandsworth kept going, walking through the castle and out into a courtyard. He stopped there, put two fingers into his mouth, and let out a loud whistle. A moment later, Chatterbox alighted from the sky and landed in the courtyard. He towered over the kids and the wizard, puffing out clouds of purple smoke.

"Catterbox!" the two Arthurs shouted.

The dragon leaned down and looked at them. The little boys patted his head.

"I think he likes you," Wandsworth said, not unkindly. "That's good."

"How is he going to help us get home?" Max asked.

"Are we going to ride him?" one of the Charlies asked.

"All dragons are related," Wandsworth said. "And they're all magic, of course. How did that Wish Eater of yours work?"

"We wrote our wishes down and fed them to it," said Tamyra.

"Then we'll try that," Wandsworth said. "I'm sure I have some paper and a quill in here somewhere." He stuck his hand into his enormous beard. There was a lot of rustling as a dozen spiders scurried out, and then he pulled out a goose feather and a piece of parchment. He handed them to Max.

"What should I say?" Max asked Tamyra. "I don't want to make things worse."

"With spells, it's best to keep them simple," Wandsworth suggested. "Especially when it comes to dragons. They can't read very well, you know."

"How about 'I wish that everything was back to the way it should be'?" Tamyra said.

Max looked at Wandsworth. "Will that undo all the crazy things that have happened?"

The wizard shrugged. "Only one way to find out."

Max looked at Tamyra, then at her brothers and sisters standing behind her. If everything went back to the way it was before, they wouldn't exist anymore. "Are you sure?" he asked her.

Tamyra hesitated a moment. Then she nodded. "I think it's the right thing to do. I won't remember anyway."

Max wrote the words out on the parchment. "Now what?" he asked Wandsworth.

"Feed it to Chatterbox," the wizard said. "That's how the other one worked, right?"

Max held the parchment up. Chatterbox leaned down and sniffed it. Then he opened his mouth, took the parchment between his teeth, and started to chew. He swallowed it with a big gulp, then belched, filling the air with purple smoke.

Max sputtered and coughed, waving his hands around to clear the smoke. When it did, he found he was sitting up in his own bed, in his own room. It was morning. In the other bed, Charlie was sitting up, yawning and stretching.

"I had the best dream," Charlie said. "We were at the Enchanted Castle."

Max got out of bed and went into the hall-way. The door to the twins' room was open, and from inside he could hear them arguing about which team's jerseys they should wear that day. Then his mother appeared, carrying Arthur.

"Oh, good. You're up," she said. "Would you mind helping Arthur get dressed? Your father hit the snooze button *four* times, and now we're running late."

"No problem," Max said, taking Arthur from her. "What do you want to wear today, buddy?" he asked his brother.

"Catterbox shirt!" Arthur said.

"You got it," said Max, taking him into his room.

The rest of the morning was chaotic, as everyone jostled for space in the bathroom and rushed through breakfast before heading off to work and school. For once, Max enjoyed every second of the craziness. He didn't even complain when Charlie knocked his milk over into his lap and he had to change his jeans.

As he was getting his books together, he got a text from Tamyra. Everything okay there?

Yep, he texted back. U?

Great!!! Tamyra replied.

On the walk to school, Max thought about what they should do with the Wish Eater. It was too dangerous to keep around. He didn't want one of his brothers or sisters finding it and accidentally wishing they could fly or asking for a talking pony or something. But he wasn't sure what should be done with it.

He forgot all about it when they got to school, and he saw Tamyra standing out front with her Charlie and her Elfie and Elsie. His heart sank. "I thought you said everything was great," he said.

"What do you mean?" Tamyra said. "It is."

"But . . . they're still here," Max whispered, nodding at her brother and sisters.

"Um, yeah," Tamyra said, looking confused. "Why wouldn't they be?"

Max started to say something more. Then it dawned on him. Tamyra didn't remember that she hadn't always had brothers and sisters. She thought they had always been there. He thought about what she'd wished—that everything would be the way it *should* be. Apparently, the Wish Eater had decided that she needed a bigger family. The fact that she didn't remember not having them before was a little frightening, and for a moment Max wondered what else the Wish Eater might have changed.

"What do you think we should do with the Wish Eater?" he asked her.

"It's not at my house," Tamyra said. "I thought maybe it would be at yours, since you bought it first."

"Uh-uh," said Max. "Maybe it went back to where it came from."

They walked into the school, where Max was immediately surrounded by Amber, Pihu, and Ji-woo.

"You'd better have memorized the cheers," Pihu said.

"You too," Ji-woo said to Tamyra. "The whole school is going to be watching."

The three girls ran off, leaving Max alone with Tamyra. Tamyra grinned. "I'm on the squad!" she said, pumping her fist.

"But I—" Max said.

"Hey," Tamyra said. "The Wish Eater knows best."

Max groaned. "Go Badgers," he said.

KEY HUNTERS

UNLOCK THE ADVENTURE... ONE KEY AT A TIME!